SUSAN EADDY

ROSALINDE BONNET

Poppy's

~~Best~~ Worst Babies*

Charlesbridge

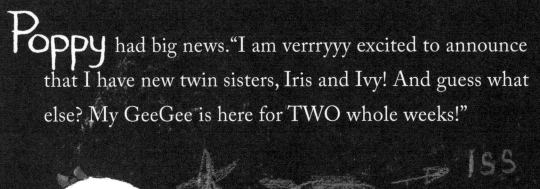

Poppy had big news. "I am verrryyy excited to announce that I have new twin sisters, Iris and Ivy! And guess what else? My GeeGee is here for TWO whole weeks!"

Lavender chimed in, "Poppy and her grandmother make the best crafts together."

Petunia said, "I bet GeeGee will be so wrapped up with Iris and Ivy that she'll ignore you."

Poppy rushed home.
"GeeGee!" she cried.

"Hello, my PoppyCakes!"

Daddy was holding the twins.
Mama and Herb were going out.

They're so cute I could eat them up.

Hello, Ivy Noodle.
Hello, Iris Tootle.

"GeeGee, let's make puppets!"
said Poppy.
GeeGee tugged Poppy's ears.
"Oh, PoppyDrop, I need to
help with the babies," she said.

Poppy found Mr. Fuzz Dog.
"We can make our own puppets," she said.
"Too bad GeeGee has to miss out."

Mama and Daddy were not at supper. But GeeGee was.

"Oh boy! I hope you made your Root Beer Carrots," said Poppy.

"Oh, Popster, twin duty took so long that I made Rutabaga Rice instead."

At bedtime Poppy asked GeeGee
to read her favorite book.

Suddenly, the giant squid's tentacles curled
around the mast and . . . and . . .

GeeGee fell asleep at the best part!

The next day Mrs. Rose rang the Ringy Thing for show-and-tell.

Poppy jumped up. "I made these puppets ALL by myself. Nobody even helped me."

"Because everybody was too busy with those babies,"
said Petunia.
Poppy scowled.

When Poppy got home, GeeGee had carrot coins waiting. GeeGee said, "Eat up, and we'll make kazoos after your snack."

Oh boy!

"It's okay. Your mama can handle it," said GeeGee.

GeeGee tugged Poppy's ears and said, "I'd better help."

"Those are the worst babies," Poppy muttered.

She and Herb made kazoos. Without GeeGee.

"Look, GeeGee," said Poppy, "we made a kazoo for you!"
But GeeGee didn't have an extra hand for a kazoo.
She whispered, "Your mama is napping, and I'm trying to
get the babies to sleep. Maybe you could kazoo a lullaby."

Poppy was not in the mood for a lullaby.

"Poppy!" said GeeGee. "Could you PLEASE keep it down?"
No, she could NOT keep it down. She marched to her room,
blowing her kazoo trombone all the way.

The next day on the bus, Lavender asked, "Are you having fun with GeeGee?"

"Yes," Poppy fibbed. "Want to come over and make potato prints with us?"

"Sure," said Lavender.

"Too many babies around there for me," said Petunia.

Poppy and Lavender got off at Poppy's house.
"PoppyCakes! Lavender Love!" said GeeGee. "Are you
ready for a potato-print-palooza?"

GeeGee cut potatoes.

Poppy and Lavender squiggled.

Poppy and Lavender stamped.

Poppy covered her ears.

"I'm sorry, Tater-Tootles," said GeeGee. "But you two go ahead. Stamp away!"

Poppy stamped away.

She stamped away on the table.

She stamped away on the rug.

She stamped away on the wall.

She was just stamping away on a
chair when GeeGee came back.

GeeGee took Lavender home.

Poppy scrubbed away.

"Not fair," Poppy told Mr. Fuzz Dog.

At supper Herb got the pirate plate, and Poppy got
the stupid clown plate.

GeeGee served squash casserole.
Poppy didn't take one bite.
GeeGee didn't even notice.

After supper GeeGee said, "PoppyDoodle, after I put the babies to bed, why don't we make Crispy Monsters?"

Poppy waited.

And waited.

And waited some more.

Finally . . .

Poppy measured. Poppy poured.

Poppy spilled. Poppy stuck.

Poppy wiped.

Poppy pulled.

"Poppy! What is going on here?!" GeeGee cried.

Poppy stomped.

Worst babies!

She stomped again and threw her spoon.

Worst Grandma!

Poppy J. Thistleberry!

Go to your room.

You have some thinking to do!

Poppy went to her room.

She did some thinking.

She thought about **Poppy J. Thistleberry!**
Not PoppyCakes? Not PoppyDoodle?
Poppy J. Thistleberry?

She cried.

She thought about the WORST babies and the WORST Grandma. She cried some more.

She thought about flying spoons and GeeGee's face and her tiny baby sisters. She sobbed.

And thought some more. Then she had an idea.

After school the next day, Poppy and Lavender went to
Poppy's room. They stamped away.

While GeeGee was busy with the babies, Lavender and
Poppy worked in the kitchen.

The next morning at recess, Poppy handed out invitations to everybody.

Even Petunia.

That evening at Poppy's house, the doorbell rang. It was Mrs. Rose!
And Lavender's family and Petunia's family and more and more.

Meet the Best Babies and
the Best Grandmother
in the whole world!
Snacks, music, and a puppet show!

Poppy and Lavender played kazoos while
Petunia and Herb put on a puppet show.
Everyone got Crispy Monster treats.

Welcome,
Iris, Ivy, and GeeGee!

Daddy swung Poppy up, and Mama kissed her on the way down.

When Iris went "Wah! Wah!" Mrs. Rose picked her up.

When Ivy went "Mah! Mah!" Lavender's daddy calmed her down.

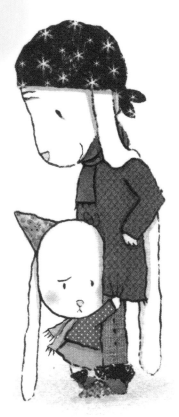

Poppy gave GeeGee a shy hug. "I don't want to be the worst big sister," she said. GeeGee tugged Poppy's ears. "Best or worst, you will always be my special PoppyDoodle," she said.

And Poppy beamed a verrrryyy huge smile.

For Jan and her ideas; for Mary, Meridth, Amanda, Jessica, and Lynne for their honesty; and for the very best twins, Julia and Susannah—S. E.

For Anne-Marie—R. B.

Published by Charlesbridge, 85 Main Street, Watertown, MA 02472 • (617) 926-0329 • www.charlesbridge.com

Library of Congress Cataloging-in-Publication Data
Names: Eaddy, Susan, author. | Bonnet, Rosalinde, illustrator.
Title: Poppy's best babies / Susan Eaddy; illustrated by Rosalinde Bonnet.
Description: Watertown, MA: Charlesbridge, [2018] | Summary: At first Poppy is thrilled by her twin baby sisters and delighted that her grandmother has come to help—but soon she finds that the two babies are taking up all the adults' time and energy, and she starts to feel angry and neglected.
Identifiers: LCCN 2017028983 (print) | LCCN 2017036743 (ebook) | ISBN 9781632896292 (ebook) | ISBN 9781632896308 (ebook pdf) | ISBN 9781580897709 (reinforced for library use)
Subjects: LCSH: Infants—Juvenile fiction. | Sisters—Juvenile fiction. | Twins—Juvenile fiction. | Grandmothers—Juvenile fiction. | Grandparent and child—Juvenile fiction. | Jealousy in children—Juvenile fiction. | CYAC: Babies—Fiction. | Sisters—Fiction. | Twins—Fiction. | Grandmothers—Fiction. | Jealousy—Fiction. | Rabbits—Fiction. | Animals—Fiction.
Classification: LCC PZ7.E1117 (ebook) | LCC PZ7.E1117 Pl 2018 (print) | DDC [E]—dc23
LC record available at https://lccn.loc.gov/2017028983

Printed in China
(hc) 10 9 8 7 6 5 4 3 2 1

Illustrations made with India ink, printing, watercolor, collage, and pencil on Arches cold-pressed watercolor paper
Hand-lettering by Rosalinde Bonnet; display type set in Canvas Inline; text type set in Adobe Caslon
Color separations by Colourscan Print Co Pte Ltd, Singapore
Printed by 1010 Printing International Limited in Huizhou, Guangdong, China
Production supervision by Brian G. Walker
Designed by Susan Mallory Sherman